RICKY AND BUSTER

WRITTEN BY KATHERINE RAWSON • ILLUSTRATED BY MICHAEL CHESWORTH

CONTENTS

PIONEER VALLEY EDUCATIONAL PRESS, INC.

Chapter One • A Birthday Surprise

"What do you want for your birthday?" Ricky's parents asked Ricky.

"I want a pet," said Ricky.

"A cat or a dog?" asked Ricky's father.

"Not a cat or a dog," said Ricky.

"A fish?" asked his mother.

"I don't think so," said Ricky.

"What about a turtle?" said his father.

"No, something different," said Ricky.

"Well, we'll see," said his mother.

When Ricky's birthday came,

he woke up early.

It was still dark outside.

Was his new pet waiting for him?

He jumped out of bed and ran to look.

Something big was on the kitchen table.

It was covered with a blanket.

What could it be?

Slowly, Ricky lifted a corner

of the blanket. He saw two pink feet

and a bright green tail.

Then he heard a loud squawk!

Ricky pulled the blanket away,
and there was a large green parrot
sitting in a cage.

"Happy birthday, Ricky!" said his parents
as they came into the room.

"Thank you! Thank you!"
  said Ricky, hugging his parents.

"This is a very special bird,"
  said Ricky's mother.
"He's very smart, and he can
  learn to talk."

"He's the best birthday present ever!"
  said Ricky.

CHAPTER TWO • BUSTER'S LESSONS

Ricky named his parrot Buster.
Every day he played with Buster
and taught him to do tricks.

Ricky taught Buster to sit on his hand
and to ring a bell.

He taught Buster to swing on a swing
and to climb a ladder.

Buster was a very smart bird.

He learned every trick

that Ricky taught him.

He learned every trick except one.

Buster wouldn't learn to talk.

"Come on, Buster, say *pretty bird*,"
Ricky begged.
But Buster was silent.

So Ricky tried to teach Buster
something else.
"Hello, Buster! Hello, Buster!"
he said over and over.
But Buster kept his beak shut.

Buster didn't say anything.
He didn't say, "Good morning."
He didn't say, "Good night."
He didn't even say,
"Give me a cracker."
Not one word came out of his beak.

Every day after school,

Ricky ran to his room

to play with Buster and to try to teach him

to talk. Every day Ricky's father said,

"Do your homework first."

"OK, Dad," Ricky said.

But he was busy showing Buster

how to hang upside down,

and he forgot.

Every evening Ricky's mother
reminded him, "Do your homework."

"Right away, Mom," Ricky said.
But he was busy trying to make Buster
say *I want a cookie*,
and he forgot.

Every day Ricky's parents said,
"Do your homework."
But every day Ricky was busy
showing Buster new tricks
and trying to teach him new words.
And every day he forgot
all about his homework.
His grades in school
got worse and worse.

One day Ricky's teacher
called his parents.
They had a long talk.

Then Ricky's parents talked to Ricky.
"We know you love Buster,"
they said, "but you have
to do your homework.
You can't play with Buster
until your grades get better."

Sadly, Ricky went to his room.
Buster was hanging upside down
from the light.

"I'm sorry, Buster," Ricky said.
"We can't play now.
I have to do my homework."

Sadly, Ricky got his books
out of his book bag.
Sadly, he sharpened his yellow pencils.
Sadly, he started
on his reading homework.

Buster watched him from the light.

Ricky was sad, but Buster was angry.

Buster wanted to play.

"Do your homework!"

squawked Buster suddenly.

"What?!" said Ricky.

"Do your homework!"
squawked Buster again,
swinging back and forth on the light.

"Buster! You talked!" shouted Ricky.

So Ricky opened his book
and began to read.
"A is for apple," he read.
"B is for bird."

"Pretty bird!" said Buster.

"C is for cookie," Ricky read.

"I want a cookie!" said Buster.

So Ricky did his homework
and Buster learned to talk.
Then they both got to play.